SNOW AND ICE

by Stephen Krensky
Pictures by John Hayes

SCHOLASTIC INC.

New York   Toronto   London   Auckland   Sydney

ISBN 0-590-41449-6

12 11 10 9 8 7 6 5 4   2 3 4/9

Printed in the U.S.A.   23
First Scholastic printing, January 1989

For Jack Frost
—S.K.

What does snow make you think of?
Sledding and skiing.
Snowmen and snowballs.

What does ice make you think of?
Slipping and skating.
Ice cubes and icicles.

Snow and ice are different things.
But they are both made of frozen water.

Snow is made of tiny water drops in the air.

When it is warm outside, these water drops
fall to the ground as rain.

When the temperature falls near 32° F (0° C),
the drops start to harden and stick
together.
This mushy stuff is *sleet.*

When the temperature goes below 32° F (0° C),
water drops freeze into tiny ice crystals.
They become snowflakes.

All snow does not look the same.
Powdery snowflakes look like sugar.
Wet snowflakes look like oatmeal.

Snowflakes have six sides.
Some of them have pointed ends.
Some of them have flat ends.

If it snows where you live,
collect some snowflakes on a piece of black
paper.
Look at them with a magnifying glass.
If you put the paper in the freezer
overnight, the snowflakes will last longer
when you are outside.

Can you count six sides on each snowflake?

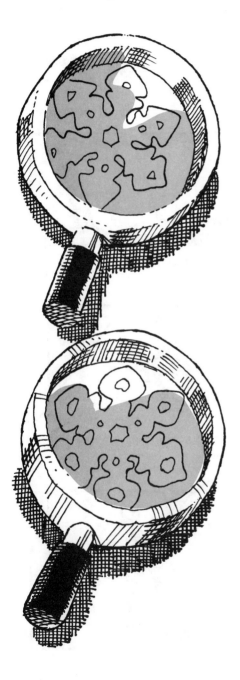

You can make your own snowflake, too. You will need

some paper,   a pencil,   and a pair of scissors.

Get some white construction paper and a
plate or a plastic container top.

Trace around it with your pencil.

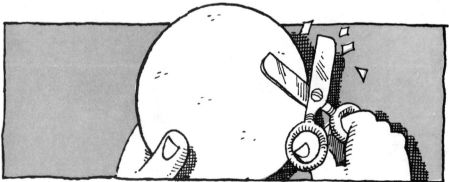

Carefully cut out the circle.

1. Fold the circle in half.

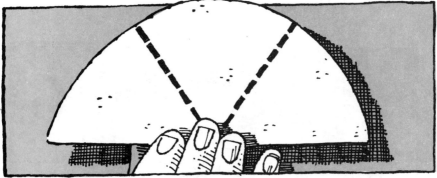

2. Then fold it again into three equal pie-shaped parts. Now your snowflake will have exactly six sides.

3. Holding the folded parts together, cut designs along the edges. You can make all kinds of snowflakes.

Snowflakes are very light.
In a strong wind they swirl all around,
often settling in huge piles called *drifts.*

A big and windy snowstorm is called a
blizzard.

A blizzard can drop several feet of snow in
one day.
Parts of Washington State once got 89 feet
of snow in just one winter.

Weather forecasters use special equipment to
measure a snowfall.
You can do it, too, with only a ruler.
If it snows where you live, try to measure
the snowfall.
Find the flattest part of the ground.
Watch out for snow drifts.
You don't want to measure one by mistake.

Stick a ruler or yardstick into the snow
until it touches the ground.
How much snow has fallen?

Although snow is cold,
fallen snow covers the ground like a blanket.
Plants and small animals that live
underground are protected by the snow from
the wind and cold.

See how this works. Get two thermometers.
Place one deep under the snow.
Place the other thermometer on top of the snow.
Leave them for a few hours.

Check the temperature on each thermometer.
They are not the same.
Which one is higher? Which one is lower?

Some animals and plants stay underground
during the winter because it's *warmer*
underneath the snow!

Hundreds of years ago, people had a hard time getting rid of the snow.
Before shovels were invented, they had to beat the snow down with their feet to make a path.

In cities, oxen pulling heavy metal rollers flattened the snow on important roads. Today, snowplows and snowblowers keep the roads clear.

The Eskimos live in the Arctic, farther
north than most other people.
Snow in the Arctic covers the ground for
hundreds of miles.
There is too much to get rid of it.

In the past, the Eskimos developed special
ways to travel.
They wore snowshoes to walk over deep snow.
When they had far to go, they rode on
dogsleds.
Today, most Eskimos in a hurry can get
around on small airplanes and snowmobiles.

In the Arctic, there is little stone or
wood for building houses.
Instead, many Eskimos use snow to build
houses called *igloos*.

First, they cut out blocks of hard-packed snow.
The blocks are placed in a circle.
As the walls rise, the roof comes together
in a dome.
Two people can build a simple igloo in a few
hours.

It takes a lot of skill to make an igloo.
But you can make a snow fort that is like an
igloo without a top.
Be sure to wear your mittens!
Get a box or crate.
Pack as much snow into it as you can.
Turn the box upside down.
Shake or tap the box until the block of snow
slides out.

Pack another box, then another.
Line up the blocks of snow.
You will have a snow fort in no time!

You can also make a snowman for the yard.
First, make a snowball.

Then roll the ball in the snow over and over
again.
This first snowball will be the largest.
It will be the bottom of your snowman.

Make a medium-sized ball for the snowman's chest
and a smaller ball for his head.
Put eyes, a nose, and a mouth on your
snowman.
You can use cookies for eyes, a carrot for
the nose, and a banana for the mouth.
To keep him warm, give him a hat and scarf.

If you pack the snow tightly when you make your snowman will last longer.
Packed snow melts more slowly than the snow on the ground.
Don't worry if the sun is shining.
The snowman may melt a little during the day, but it will freeze up again at night.

Some people carve huge mounds
of hard-packed snow into snow sculptures.
It is easier to carve out designs on packed snow than on ice.
When the sculpture is finished, it is covered with water to freeze hard.
Everyone wants the snow sculpture to last as long as possible!

Nobody has to pack down the snow in the
Arctic and Antarctica to make it last.
It is so cold there that a lot of the snow
never melts.
The Arctic is a frozen ocean surrounded by
land at the top of the earth.
The Antarctic is a frozen land surrounded by
ocean at the bottom of the earth.

Most of the snow in the Arctic and Antarctic
piles up year after year.
It gets very heavy.
It packs down tightly under its own weight.

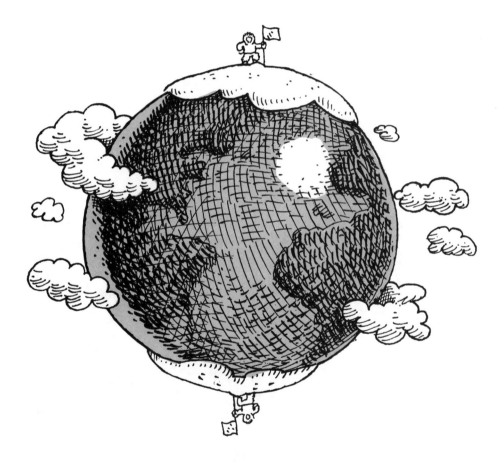

Get three containers that are the same size.
Give each one a number.

Fill #1 all the way to the top with soft snow.
Fill #2 with snow that has been tightly packed.
Fill #3 with ice.

Make sure they are filled to the same level.
Then put the containers in a warm room.
Let the snow and ice melt.
Which container has the most water?

Snow is made of tiny ice crystals that stick
together.
There is a lot of air between the ice
crystals in loose snow.
Air takes up a lot of space.
This is why loose snow contains less water
than packed snow and ice.
Air is warmer than ice crystals.
It helps the loose snow to melt quickly.
Crystals in ice are closer together than
they are in snow.
This leaves less room for air in ice.
This is why ice takes longer to melt.

As the snow in the Arctic and Antarctic
squeezes together,
some of it turns to ice.
Some Antarctic ice is three miles thick.
This ice, which spreads out over the land,
is called a *glacier.*
Over time glaciers can push boulders
hundreds of miles away,
or mow down forests like grass.

Today glaciers still cover Greenland and
Antarctica.
But at the edge of the sea,
pieces of the glaciers break off.
These pieces are called *icebergs.*

Icebergs can be white or green or blue.
Some icebergs are flat like parking lots.
One of them was measured to be 60 miles (96 km)
wide and over 200 miles (338 km) long.
Other icebergs are jagged like mountains.
Some have been 300 feet (90.1 m) tall.

Icebergs float in the water
because air is trapped inside them.
Air is much lighter than water.
Only the top of the iceberg can be seen.
Most of it stays below the surface.
If an iceberg rises 100 feet (30 m) into
the air, it probably reaches down 800 feet (262 m)
into the water.

An iceberg is something like an ice cube.
Put an ice cube in a glass of water.
How much of the ice cube sticks out above
the water? How much stays under the water?

Big icebergs are dangerous to ships.
The most famous ship to hit an iceberg was
the *Titanic*.
On its first voyage, in 1912,
the *Titanic* hit an iceberg on a foggy night.
The ship quickly sank and 1,517 people died.

For a long time everyone kept away from icebergs.
Nobody thought they were useful.
But giant icebergs are large sources of fresh water.
Some people now want to tow them to places
like Los Angeles and Saudi Arabia,
where more fresh water is needed.
The icebergs will be wrapped in plastic
to keep them from melting.

Find out how plastic helps.
Take two ice cubes out of your freezer.
Put one ice cube into a plastic bag.
Then put both ice cubes in a bowl of water.
Which ice cube melts first?

Ice is formed in different ways.
In warm places, water in lakes or rivers
freezes into ice when the temperature drops
below 32° F (0° C).
Water droplets that form on other surfaces
turn into a kind of ice we call frost.
Frost is a very thin layer of ice.
It forms on windows and sidewalks, on the
ground and on plants.

You can make frost with some ice, salt,
and a can.
Put a cup of crushed ice and one-half cup of
rock salt in a can.
Water from the air will slowly collect
on the outside of the can.
In about one hour, this water will harden
into frost.

All fresh water freezes into ice.
But dripping water freezes in a special way.
It freezes drop by drop into an icicle.
As the water drops slide down, the icicle
gets longer and longer.

CLOUD

RAIN

SNOW

ROOF

MELT
MELT
MELT

ICICLES

Icicles hang from trees, from cars, and from
the roofs of houses and buildings.
Where does the water come from when an
icicle forms on the edge of a roof?

Oceans do not freeze in the winter, partly
because they contain salt.
Saltwater must get much colder than fresh
water to freeze.

The oceans usually don't get this cold.
You can see how this works.
Get two containers.   Fill both with water.
Add two tablespoons of salt to one container.

Mark this container with an S.
Leave the containers in the freezer for two hours.
The container without the salt is frozen.
What about the other one?

Salt helps keep ice away.
It can be dangerous to walk or drive on ice.
When you walk on ice, your foot can slip
and slide.

When ice collects on roads, cars slide, too.
So trucks spread sand or salt on snowy roads
to keep ice from forming.

The tops of ponds and lakes also freeze in
the cold.
But they never freeze all the way to the bottom.
Some fish keep swimming under ice.
If you go ice-skating on a frozen pond,
watch out for thin ice.
You don't want to fall in and join the fish.

When you ice-skate, you are actually skating
on water, not ice.
The pressure and movement of your blade on
the ice makes the ice under the blade melt.
You slide on a thin layer of water whenever
you put your skates down on the ice.

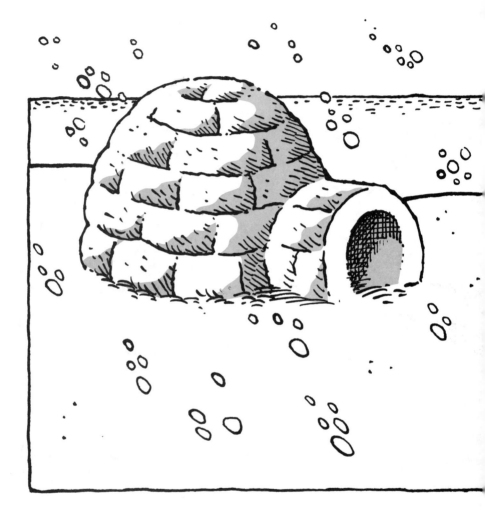

Blizzards and igloos,

icebergs and frozen ponds

— snow and ice come in many forms.
They can be helpful or dangerous.
They can also be a lot of fun.
When you play on snow or ice,
wear warm clothes,
and don't forget the carrot for the
snowman's nose!